To my grandma

First Edition, September 2016
10 9 8 7 6 5 4 3 2 1
FAC-029191-16135

Printed in Malaysia

Library of Congress Cataloging-in-Publication Data

Names: Kang, A. N.
Title: The very fluffy kitty, Papillon / A. N. Kang.
Description: First edition. | Los Angeles ; New York : Disney HYPERION, 2016.
| Summary: Papillon is a cat who is so fluffy he floats, so his owner tries many silly ways to keep him on the ground.
Identifiers: LCCN 2015019786| ISBN 9781484717981 | ISBN 1484717988
Subjects: | CYAC: Cats—Fiction. | Humorous stories.
Classification: LCC PZ7.1.K26 Ve 2016 | DDC [E]—dc23
LC record available at http://lccn.loc.gov/2015019786
Reinforced binding
Visit www.DisneyBooks.com

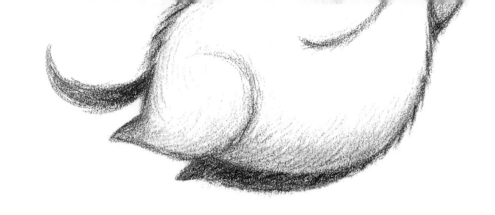

THE VERY FLUFFY KITTY

Papillon

BY A. N. KANG

Disney • HYPERION

Los Angeles   New York

Papillon is a big kitty.

He is not fat.

Just very fluffy.

I mean FLUFFY!

He is lighter than air,

which can get him into trouble.

PAPILL

WHERE ARE YOU??

Papillon lives with Miss Tilly.

She loves him so much! She is always worried that Papillon could float away and get lost.

In the beginning, Miss Tilly tried to weigh him down with yummy treats: doughnuts, fish, pizza.

Nothing worked.

Until finally, something did.

Miss Tilly started out simple,

but then she got carried away.

Papillon did not like wearing clothes.
One day, he refused. Cats are like that.

WHAT ABOUT A HAT?

JUST AN EYE PATCH?

Miss Tilly soon gave up and left for the market. Papillon had a lot of fun that afternoon.

There was synchronized swimming, a relaxing nap, acrobatics, a sing-along to his favorite tune and, of course, dancing.

Then he noticed a new friend!
Papillon wanted to say hello.

But the bird flew away.

Where did he go?
Papillon followed his friend.

Soon, he was lost.

No one seemed as
sweet as Miss Tilly.
He wanted to go home.

Papillon didn't know the way.

He took a rest to think.
He made himself a hat,
a scarf, and a belt.

But they didn't work as well as
the outfits Miss Tilly had made.
Papillon did not know what to do.

But his new friend did!

The pair made their way home.

> I WAS SO WORRIED!
> WHO IS THIS ON YOUR HEAD?
> HMMM...

Miss Tilly had a new idea.

Papillon didn't mind
the new hat at all.